Stowaway!

Written by Julia Jarman

Illustrated by Mark Oldroyd

Collins

1. Decision time!

It was a cold November afternoon and a wind had got up. Dickon looked longingly at the ships in Plymouth harbour, five of them, white sails billowing. There was the *Marigold*, the *Benedict*, the *Swan*, the *Elizabeth* and the flagship, the *Pelican*.

How Dickon envied his best friend, Tib, who was aboard the *Pelican*, for the famous Francis Drake was its captain – Francis Drake, England's greatest sailor and friend of Good Queen Bess. Francis Drake who had come back from the Spanish Main, his ship laden with gold. And now he was setting out on another exciting voyage – with Tib as his cabin boy.

Dickon gritted his teeth to stop the tears. He'd tried to get a job, but the second mate had taken one look at his lame leg and said, "Sorry, lad. We only take the fit and able. You couldn't climb the mainmast."

"I could … "

But the second mate hadn't listened. Instead, he said to Tib, "You'll do. You look a strong lad." So Tib would have gold for his mother when the ship returned to Plymouth. Dickon would have nothing, and his poor widowed mother had eight boys to feed.

Dickon was suddenly jolted out of his misery by a loud voice.

"Here, boy, carry this!" A young gentleman in a leather doublet had dropped a bag at Dickon's feet.

Then a gentleman with dark hair and
beard called out from the *Pelican*.

"Cousin John! Not a moment too soon.
We sail at five!"

Dickon couldn't believe his eyes.
It was Francis Drake!
It must be. He wore
a gold chain round
his neck.

"Cousin Francis!" The young gentleman ran up the gangway. Dickon ran after him, carrying the bag. He *could* run and climb. He could do lots of things.

Francis Drake and his cousin, John, hugged each other. "Put your mattress and bag in the grand cabin, then join me," said the Captain. John Drake turned to Dickon. "Come on, lad!" Dickon followed him down the ladder eagerly, for he'd made an important decision.

Where to hide? That was the question. The hold would be best. Luckily everyone was busy loading the ship or tightening the rigging, so no one took much notice of him. Leaving John Drake in the grand cabin, Dickon headed back to the ladder as the ship started to rock. The tide was on the turn. Soon the ship would leave. He must be quick. Down the ladder he went – and down again – and again. The lower he got, the darker it got. Now he could hear men heaving cargo into place, but only see their shapes. Dodging behind the ladder, he heard someone above shout orders.

"Cast off the lines!"

He felt the ship float free. They were off! Now men scrambled over him, up the ladder. "Let's get on deck, lads! Let's see the last of old England!"

The last of old England! As Dickon wedged himself between a barrel and a bale of linen, he felt a thrill of excitement.

2. Discovered!

But later that night Dickon was scared. A storm had got up and the ship was rolling from side to side. He could hear the wind howling and feel the sea crashing against the sides. Dickon was hungry too. Where would he get food? What would happen if he were found? What if the ship sank? How would his mother know where he was? Then the ship nearly keeled over, throwing him out of his hiding place. Dickon saw a man with a swaying lantern peering down at him.

"What are you doing here, boy?"

"Hiding, sir." He was too hungry to lie.

"Captain, not sir. Don't you know the punishment for entering the hold?"

Dickon recognised the man. It was Captain Drake. He shouted at Dickon, "If you've been stealing, boy, you will have your hand nailed to the mast."

"I haven't been stealing. I wanted a job."

"And do you still?" said the captain, more gently, now.

"Yes, Captain, I want gold for my mother, so she can feed my brothers."

Now the famous man stooped to peer closely at Dickon. "Aren't you sea-sick, boy?"

"No, Captain. I'm too hungry to be sick."

Drake laughed and pulled Dickon to his feet. "There are forty men above, all as sick as pigs, except you and me. So, lad, if we survive this storm, you have a job. I just hope you like adventure."

They did survive, though the storm raged for three days. Dickon became a cabin boy to Francis Drake, along with his friend Tib.

"It's the best job on board," laughed Tib, "looking after the captain!"

Captain Drake told his crew that they were sailing to the Indies. "To get as much Spanish gold as we can! Gold for the Queen, whose blessing we have, and as revenge for the terrible things Spaniards have done to Englishmen!"

When the *Pelican* sailed past the Mediterranean Sea and turned west towards the Indies, Dickon thought of the adventure he was going to have. And when he came home, his mother would never have to worry again. He pictured himself handing her a bag of gold and the big feast they would all have!

IRELAND

ENGLAND

FRANCE

SPAIN

AFRICA

3. Mutiny ... almost!

Not everyone on the *Pelican* was happy about going to the Indies. Some of the crew grumbled when Drake ordered them to sail south-west. Their grumbles grew when for weeks there was no sight of land. Then the little fleet seemed stuck, for there was no wind, none at all. And it was hot – scorching hot – the sun was like fire. It was because they were near the line, some old hands said, the line round the middle of the world. When Dickon and Tib could bear to go on deck they couldn't see any line, just sea, huge fish and enormous birds. Sailors were dying from the heat and Preacher Fletcher was kept busy with funeral services.

As Dickon saw bodies being thrown into the sea he began to wonder if he would ever get home, and his dreams of riches began to fade.

But soon afterwards a fair wind got up and spirits rose on the *Pelican*.

"Gold *will* be ours!" Drake said in a ringing speech to the crew. "For we are on course again! We have only to get through the Magellan Straits, then we'll be in sight of Spanish galleons!"

Only get through the Magellan Straits! Dickon had heard about them. Criss-crossed by dangerous currents, they were like tunnels with mountains on either side.

Soon after his speech, Drake ordered them to dock on the east coast of Brasilia. He wanted to get repairs done before the dreaded straits. He also decided to repaint the *Pelican* in red and yellow, the colours of his backer, Sir Christopher Hatton. He renamed the ship too. From now on she was the *Golden Hinde*. The carpenter had to carve a new ship's head in the shape of a hind. Drake said they would coat it with Spanish gold as soon as they had boarded a Spanish galleon and taken all of its treasure!

As he and Tib helped paint the handrail on the upper deck, Dickon started to get a little scared again. Wasn't it unlucky to change the name of a ship? Preacher Fletcher had blessed it, but they'd still got to get through the Magellan Straits.

4. A challenge

Dickon needn't have worried. With Drake at the helm the *Golden Hinde* sailed through safely in sixteen days. The *Marigold* and the *Elizabeth* were not far behind.

"Thanks be to God!" cried Drake as they entered the South Sea. "We are the first Englishmen to come this way! And now the fun begins. The first man or boy to spy a Spanish treasure ship will get a link of this!"

He swung his gold chain above his head. There was a race for the rigging. Tib ran to the mainmast and started climbing.

Dickon ran to the foremast, shouting, "Race you to the top, Tib!"

A boy called Will ran to the mizzenmast. They all began climbing, and the crew began to clap rhythmically.

Dickon had been practising. He climbed as fast as he could, but when he was only half way Tib yelled, "First!" The crew cheered. They cheered again when Will reached the top of the mizzen. And they cheered Dickon when he reached the top of the foremast, but he couldn't help feeling disappointed. With his lame leg, would he ever be fast enough to win a link of Drake's golden chain? He scanned the horizon. There was nothing wrong with his eyes. Perhaps he would be the first to see a Spanish galleon? But all he saw was the coast stretching north as far as he could see. No ships at all.

Then Tib yelled, "Storm clouds in the south! Moving towards us! Fast!"

It was a huge bank of black cloud, moving ever so fast. They scrambled down to tell the others. An older hand agreed with them. A huge storm was on its way.

Captain Drake shouted orders.

"Batten down the hatches! Shorten the sails! Then lash yourselves to the ship!"

"Above or below?" said Tib to Dickon.

"Above," said Dickon. "I want to see it."

But when the storm came he couldn't see anything.
He could only feel icy waves crashing over him.
As darkness fell he felt the ship flying through
the water, and all he could do was pray.

5. Treasure ship sighted!

The storm lasted for thirty days: thirty days of being lashed by wind and sea with little to eat or drink. When at last it blew itself out the *Golden Hinde* was alone. A much leaner Drake looked at his charts and compasses and scanned the sea with his Bring 'em Near.

"First the bad news. We are at least fifty miles off course and there is no sign of our sister ships." Someone said he had seen the *Marigold* go down.

"But now the good news," said Drake. "We are still in the Southern Ocean, so we have made a discovery. There is no continent to the south, and," he pointed north, "that way lie the treasure ships of Spain!"

It took them a whole week to reach land – the west coast of Peru – but when they did their luck continued. Native Indians came out to welcome them ashore with food and much-needed water. Then the chief drew pictures in the sand, showing them that a Spanish ship had passed that way a week before, and that the crew had killed and injured many Indians.

"They like us because we are not cruel like the Spanish," said Drake, ordering everyone back on board. "Draw up the anchor and unfurl the sails! And," he touched his golden chain, "remember what I said!"

Dickon clambered up the mainmast this time, longing to be the first to spot the Spanish vessel. But he wasn't the first. It was Tib who saw it four days later, Tib who got the first link from the captain's golden chain. Dickon was pleased for his friend, but wondered again if *he* would ever have gold in his pocket.

His hopes were raised as Captain Drake described the plan of attack.

"We could catch up with the Spanish this day, for our little ship is much faster than their heavy vessel. But we'll be cunning and wait till night. They'll have seen us, as we've seen them, so let's make them think we're as slow as them. Hang heavy objects like mattresses and cables and iron pots over the sides to slow us down. Tonight, when they think they're moored safely miles away from us, we'll cut our tows, advance swiftly and take them by surprise.

Remember, every man or boy who boards their vessel will get a share of the spoils!"

Every man or boy! At last! Dickon thought his chance had come. But his hopes were dashed with the Captain's next words.

"You, Dickon, will stay aboard the *Golden Hinde* and help stow the stolen treasure in the hold."

Dickon could hardly believe it. He wasn't even going to board the Spanish vessel! Because of his leg, he had to stay with old or injured men, like Peter, the ship's cook.

That night, when the *Golden Hinde* crept alongside the Spanish ship, Dickon had to watch as the rest of the crew leapt aboard. But he shared the excitement when the crew came back with 25,000 golden ducats, thirteen chests of plate, eighty pounds of solid gold and twenty-six tons of silver, as well as fruit conserves and sacks of sugar!

As they sailed north other triumphs followed, for
more Spanish treasure ships were sighted and raided.
Soon the ballast rocks had to be thrown overboard,
because there was enough gold and silver in the hold
of the *Golden Hinde* to keep her steady. But still none
of the treasure was Dickon's.

6. Ambush!

Some months later, they came to a small island off the west coast of North America ... and Dickon's fortunes suddenly changed.

As he rowed ashore with Captain Drake and twenty others, Dickon expected the usual warm welcome from the natives. By now he was used to seeing painted Indians greeting them with gifts of meat and fruit. Unusually, there were none here.
Drake, scanning the island with his Bring 'em Near, said he thought the island was uninhabited. "But there are trees bearing luscious-looking fruit, and huge birds, with their heads in the sand, waiting to be eaten!"

"Ostriches," said one of the sailors, "and they are easy meat, for they cannot fly."

"I hope they taste better than penguins," laughed Drake.

When they landed, the Captain asked Dickon to hold the Bring 'em Near while he tried to catch one.

Eagerly, Dickon raised the instrument to his eye. Magic! That's what it always seemed like.

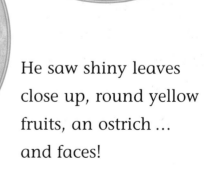

He saw shiny leaves close up, round yellow fruits, an ostrich ... and faces!

"Captain!" called Dickon. But Captain Drake, creeping up on an ostrich, didn't hear.

"What ... ?" shouted the sailor who'd first seen the ostriches. But he didn't finish his question, for he staggered backwards with an arrow in his heart.

"Indians ... " whispered Dickon, as men round him fell silently. Whoosh! Whoosh! More arrows rained from the trees.

And still the Captain hadn't noticed.

"DUCK!" Rushing forward, Dickon pushed Drake sideways as an arrow flew straight at him.

Too late! It entered Drake's cheek. Dickon managed to drag him into some undergrowth. Now some of the crew were firing arms, but others were still falling.

"Better my head than my heart," Drake rallied. "To the boat!" he cried. "As fast as you can! Let's live to fight another day!" There was no point in fighting here. Their musket fire didn't reach the Indians, whose arrows kept coming.

The Indians themselves came no nearer. They did not want to fight, just to drive the intruders away from their island.

As Dickon helped his master into the rowing boat,
the Captain said, "You saved my life, lad.
You thought of me, not yourself,
and I will not forget it."

7. Gold at last!

Drake was as good as his word. He did not forget Dickon's bravery. He rewarded him with not one, but three links of his golden chain, and something else, which he pressed into Dickon's hand.

"A ducat for your 'Duck', lad!"

A solid gold ducat!

"And there may well be more," said Captain Drake, "because there will be other treasure ships to plunder before we reach home."

Dickon had now been at sea for over a year and he longed for home. He did not know then that it would be another two years and many more adventures before he returned to England. For Francis Drake soon revealed another secret plan! He said they were not going back to England the way they had come. They were going to sail on and on, north then west.

"We are going to be the first Englishmen to sail right round the world!"

Was the world really round like a ball as some said? Dickon could hardly believe it. Wouldn't they fall off if they kept going in one direction?

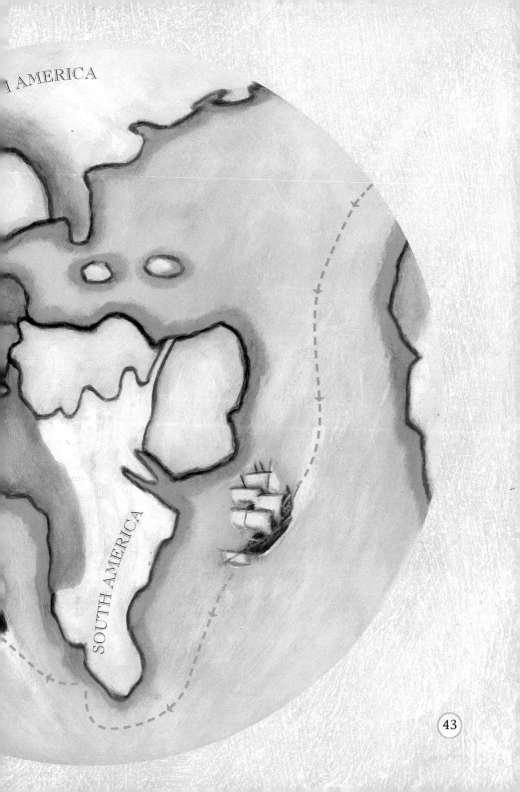

I AMERICA

SOUTH AMERICA

No! But he only truly believed it when the *Golden Hinde* sailed into Plymouth harbour on the twenty-sixth of September 1580. He was the happiest boy in the world – he was sure of it – for he had sailed round the world with the famous Francis Drake, he had Spanish gold in his pocket and his family would never be poor again!

And there was more excitement to come – for he sailed on with the *Golden Hinde* to London. They were in Deptford when Queen Elizabeth herself came aboard and knighted Drake, making him Sir Francis Drake. Dickon thought he would burst with pride when Sir Francis presented him to the queen, saying, "This is the boy who saved my life!"

Dickon's voyage

Dickon is refused a job on the *Pelican*

John Drake asks Dickon to carry his bag aboard ship

The ship is renamed the *Golden Hinde*

The *Golden Hinde* reaches Peru

The crew raids a Spanish ship

Dickon becomes a cabin boy and the ship sails to the Indies

Dickon is presented to the Queen

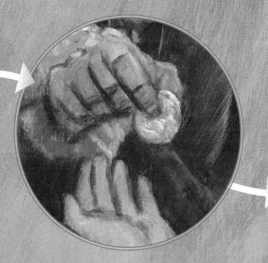

The *Golden Hinde* returns after sailing around the world

Ideas for reading

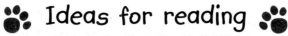

Written by Clare Dowdall PhD
Lecturer and Primary Literacy Consultant

Learning objectives: how settings and characters are built from small details; explore chronology in stories by noticing how time passes; use phonic/spelling knowledge as a cue, together with graphic, grammatical and contextual knowledge; sustain roles when carrying out a decision making task

Curriculum links: What were the effects of Tudor exploration?

Interest words: stowaway, mainmast, gangway, hold, rigging, Indies, Spaniards, Mediterranean Sea, mutiny, Magellan Straits, galleon, foremast, mizzenmast

Resources: map of the world/globe

Getting started

This book can be read over two or more guided reading sessions.

- Read the word *stowaway* together. Look for words within the word and ask them to work out what stowaway means.

- Read the blurb and look at the pictures together. Introduce the Tudor explorer Sir Francis Drake and explain that he was the first British explorer to sail all the way around the world in the 16th century. Show Drake's journey out of Plymouth and towards the Indies on the globe or map.

- Ask them to describe what they think it would be like to stowaway on a ship in Tudor times. What would they be excited about? What would be frightening or unpleasant?

- Ask them what they think will happen to Dickon.

Reading and responding

- Read pp2-5 together. Ask them to be story detectives and to list all the information about Dickon that they can infer so far.

- Remind them to use context questions to understand historical words (e.g. ask *"What could a doublet be if he is in it and it is leather?"*)